Meet The All Stars

Nick

Carlos

Carla

Flo

Juan

Kareem

Lucy

Lacy

Larry

Thank Goodness It's T-ball Day

By Kevin Christofora
Illustrated by Dale Tangeman

As much as Dale and I were excited to jump into *Pizza Pie Day*, the reality of "keeping it real" was of utmost importance. You really can't play in the field and make throws to first base if you don't know how to throw. *TGIT* is exactly what the doctor ordered. *TGIT* was inspired by the actual technique of the kids looking like a letter "T" to learn how to throw. Most parents relate to T.G.I.F.—now, kids can look forward to two days!

I dedicate this book to a few specific people without whom these books would still be on my dining room table as just my big idea: Ric Aliberte, Michael Reinert, Brittany Bearden, Kelly Hashway, Simon Rose, Brian Mast, Jeff Bearden and Clarens Publishing.

CLARENS PUBLISHING

1. Children's 2. Sports 3. Baseball 4. Non-Fiction 5. Educational 6. Historical 7. T-ball 8. Woodstock 9. TGIF

Library of Congress Control Number: 2015960086

ISBN 978-0-9863493-2-4

Printed in the United States of America

What a beautiful, warm and sunny day with big fluffy clouds. I couldn't wait for baseball practice today.

Every day before we went home, while we waited for the buses, Kareem loved to pretend he was playing guitar. Everyone liked to watch, because he was so funny.

When we got home, we ran off the bus, because the sooner we got our homework done, the sooner we could play baseball.

Today, Kareem got to ride the bus home with us, because his parents had to work late. We were going to carpool to practice.

While we all did our homework, Mom made my favorite snack— apple wedges with peanut butter to dip them in.

5

We were so excited to get to practice. Coach told us to put our water bottles on the bench and line up on the fence.

"Come on, Kareem. We are not playing Spiderman today," Coach said. "It is time to play baseball!"

TEAM ROSTER

Carlos................Catcher

Flo................Pitcher

Carla................Left Field

Nick................Short Stop

Ju................First Base

K................Second Base

................Center Field

................Third

................Ri

Coach said, "Great! I am glad you liked batting. Now, I want to tell you a little story about another legend of the game. Cy Young was known for being one of the best-ever pitchers in baseball. Did you know that you can't pitch until you learn how to throw? Today, we are going to learn how to throw, and, maybe one day you can be a pitcher just like Cy Young."

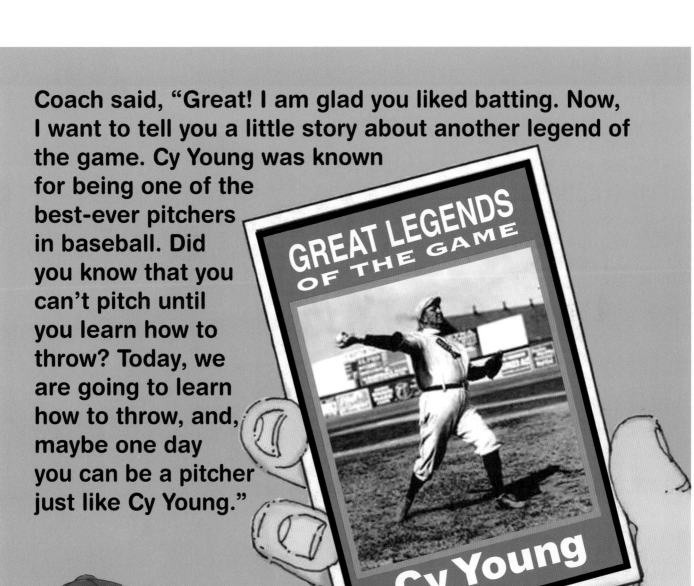

GREAT LEGENDS OF THE GAME

Cy Young

Cy Young was one of the first pitchers to get into the Baseball Hall of Fame, which is a baseball museum in Cooperstown, New York. Everyone who lives there loves baseball. Even the ice cream man!

Flo raised her hand.
"Yes, Flo?" Coach asked. "What is it?"

"Can we do our warm-ups now?"
she replied.

Coach smiled. "Oh, yes! Thank you. I was so excited to show you my baseball card I almost forgot. Yes, yes, yes. You're the leader. Take 'em out!"

Flo took us to the pitcher's mound, where we always did our warm-ups. She was a very good leader.

"Ready? Pencil...rocket, pencil...rocket. Let's do ten!

"Helicopters...Remember to keep your feet together. Let's do ten!"

"On your tippy toes—reach for the moon, and down. Let's do ten!"

Flo handed the white hat to Carlos. Now, he was the leader. "Let's do two laps around the bases. Don't forget to yell the name of the base when you step on it," Carlos said.

We all ran around. When Kareem got close to home plate, he was singing, "Peanut butter jelly, peanut butter jelly, peanut butter jelly with a baseball bat," as he continued to dance across home plate.

At the throwing station, everyone put their feet in the circles and Coach said, "Notice that you are all facing me, not the target."

First, we stood like a letter "T". Next, we pointed our gloves at our target.

"Rock back toward the ball," Coach said. "Rock forward, and throw over the top."

17

"No spaghetti arms!" Coach said. "Keep your arms straight and way over your head when you throw. Like a windmill!"

"What is that?" I asked. Coach laughed and said, "Let me explain."

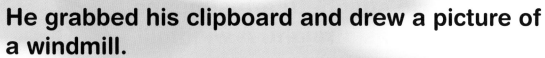

He grabbed his clipboard and drew a picture of a windmill.

I was so excited to practice to get better at throwing. At the end of the school year, Mr. Bono, our school principal, was going to sit in the dunk tank. I wanted to make him fall in the water...so bad!

We had a fun practice. Coach told us that throwing was one of the most important skills we needed to learn to play baseball. "You were all awesome today," Coach said. "What was your favorite part?"

Coach started laughing and said, "That's enough spaghetti for one day. Let's go to the bleachers!"

These questions were always my favorite part. I was even practicing with Kareem on the bus ride home.

Shout It Out!

1. What is the name of the game?.........................

2. Why do we play it?.........................

3. What is your favorite day of the week?................

4. Who likes peanut butter and jelly with a baseball bat?.........................

5. If you get 3 strikes, you are ____?.........................

6. Who was the best hitter ever?.........................

7. Who was the best pitcher ever?.........................

8. Where is the Baseball Hall of Fame?................

9. Who thinks they can dunk Mr. Bono?................

1. Baseball 2. To have fun 3. Tuesday and/or Thursday 4. Me 5. Out 6. Babe Ruth 7. Cy Young 8. Cooperstown 9. Me

While Coach had us all on the bleachers, he said, "Before I ask you all the last question, I want to show you these. They are wristbands with three different sayings on them.

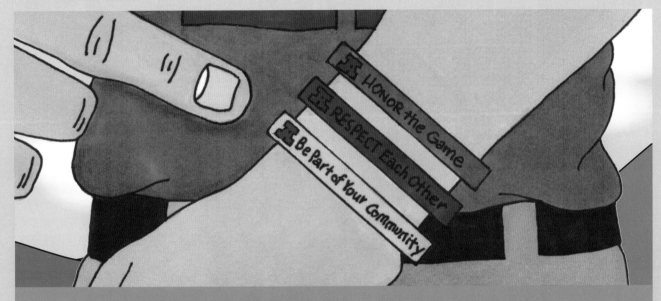

HONOR The Game means to remember and respect legends like Babe Ruth and Cy Young.
RESPECT Each Other means that you are nice to your friends and teammates.
Be Part Of Your COMMUNITY means shop in your hometown and thank the businesses that support your team. It helps to build community spirit."

Coach then said, "Alright! Now the last question... who wants a wristband?" We all got to pick one color wristband and, of course, Coach gave everyone a fruit pop.

We had such a fun day. I was sad it was over. I couldn't wait for another T-Day of the week.

Here are some words we have learned in this book. See if you can find them in the word puzzle below.

Hey, kids. How many times does the baseball stealing gopher appear in this book? Answer is at the bottom of this page.

Tuesday

Thursday

Pitch

Throw

Dancing

Windmill

Spaghetti

Carpool

Respect

Honor

Community

Cooperstown

EXTRA INNINGS

How many other All Star words can you find? Fun, Nick, Ball, Home, Hat, Base, Bat, Coach, AllStars, Peanut Butter, Jelly, Catch, Glove, Foul, TGIT

F	U	N	N	I	C	K	B	A	L	L	H	O	M	E
B	A	T	T	H	U	R	S	D	A	Y	R	I	J	R
P	I	T	C	H	H	O	N	O	R	H	A	T	E	E
F	B	C	A	S	P	A	G	H	E	T	T	I	L	S
P	E	A	N	U	T	B	U	T	T	E	R	P	L	P
D	T	R	C	U	M	P	T	U	E	S	D	A	Y	E
A	H	P	A	S	T	G	I	T	K	E	L	L	Y	C
N	R	O	T	L	C	O	M	M	U	N	I	T	Y	T
C	O	O	C	F	O	U	L	H	C	O	A	C	H	B
I	W	L	H	A	L	L	S	T	A	R	S	U	M	A
N	G	L	O	V	E	W	I	N	D	M	I	L	L	S
G	C	O	O	P	E	R	S	T	O	W	N	K	E	E

Answer: 10 times, including the gopher taking a nap

Hey Kids, look for more
Hometown All Stars books
at a bookstore near you.

Get Free Baseball Cards!

Tell us what your favorite part of baseball practice was, or draw
a picture and mail it to us with a self addressed stamped envelope to:
The Hometown All Stars P.O. Box 235, Woodstock, New York, 12498.

Join the Team! Just because you finished the book,
doesn't mean the Hometown All Stars fun stops!
Team gear, interactive games and contests, nutrition tips,
a free coloring book, and more are all on our website!

www.thehometownallstars.com